UNKNOWN
The Slasher

By

Bradley Talmadge Livingston

Dedication

"To you, dear reader, for making this journey worthwhile."

"For my readers, who breathe life into these pages."

"To all who pick up this book, thank you for giving my words a chance." "For every reader who finds a piece of themselves within these chapters."

In loving memory of my grandmother Pearlie Mae Mumford (1932–2021).

Acknowledgment

My mother is an amazing woman. I find it difficult to say what she means to me in just a few sentences. I thank my mom for bringing me into this world no other gift can bear. I was disciplined by a woman named Virgie Mae Saunders(Stoner) and a grandmother named Pearlie Mae Mumford, who taught me right from wrong each and every day to make something out of my life. (Psalms 19:1; Romans 1:20)

Contents

Dedication...iii

Acknowledgment iv

About the Author..ix

Chapter 1 1

49 Strangest Unsolved Mysteries 7

1.The Body on Somerton Beach................................ 7

2. The Strange Disappearance of D.B. Cooper................. 8

3. The Black Dahlia Murder 10

4. Wall Street Bombing of 1920................................12

5. The Disturbing Death of Elisa Lam........................ 14

6. Jack the Ripper 15

7. The Zodiac Killer 16

8. The Case of JonBenét Ramsey 18

9. Chicago Tylenol Murders 20

10. The Unsolved Hinterkaifeck Murders 21

11. The Ghost Ship of the Mary Celeste 23

12. The Watcher House..24

13. The Mystery of the Circleville Letters 26

14. The Sodder Children Disappearance 27

15. The Axeman of New Orleans...................................... 30

16. The Death of the Boy in the Box 32

17. The Mysterious Drowning of Natalie Wood, Robert Wagner and Natalie Wood 33

18. The Keddie Cabin Murders...................................... 36

19. The Gardner Museum Heist...................................... 37

20. The Disappearance of Jimmy Hoffa in 1966 39

21. The Eight-Day Bride 42

22. The Creepy Murder in Room 1046 44

23. The Shark Arm Murders 48

24. The Lost Colony of Roanoke..................................... 50

25. The Disappearance of Dorothy Arnold 51

26. The Murder of Bugsy Siegel 52

27. The Jamison Family Disappearance.......................... 55

28. The O.J. Simpson Case 57

29. The Mystery of Overtoun Bridge 60

30. Malaysia Airlines Flight 370 Disappearance 61

31. The Peculiar Death of Charles C. Morgan 62

32. The Disappearance of Walter Collins........................64

33. The Unexplained Phoenix Lights 67

34. The Eerie Lady of the Dunes 69

35. The Case of Mary Reeser.....................................71

36. Escape from Alcatraz 73

37. The Sheppard Murder Case....................................76

38. The Killing of Ken Rex McElroy 79

39. The Michelle Von Emster Case................................ 83

40. The Pollock Sisters..86

41. The Disappearance of Paula Jean Welden.................88

42. The Disappearance of the Flannan Isles Lighthouse Keepers...90

43. The Murder of Betty Shanks 92

44. The Leatherman.. 93

45. The Severed Feet Mystery 94

46. The Case of Jeanette DePalma 95

47. The Vanishing of Cynthia Anderson.........................96

48. The Disappearance of Kyron Horman......................99

49. The Bizarre Deaths at Dyatlov Pass 100

About the Author

Bradley Livingston is a 12 1/2-year US Army & Army National Guard veteran who served and wants to inspire the whole world and the horror story in his own way. He also has a new homeschool offered online for the convenience of your home to provide students with a safer environment. The school is called Bradley T Livingston High School College and Bradley T. Livingston High School for the Arts, and it is the home of the Taipans.

Chapter 1

Once upon a time, there was a man who was all alone in a house where he was living with a demonic witch who was satan's child. On the night of March 25, 2023, all hell broke loose. He was fixing his dinner, hotdogs, and fries when the demonic witch threatened to frame him for crimes he had not committed and report the police to remove him from the house. The time was 9:30 p.m.

The man said, "Only God and the Lord Jesus Christ know of the beast."

This outraged the demonic witch, who grabbed the man violently with his arm. The demonic witch was no ordinary woman as she fell to the floor, seething with anger.

Looking at her, the man thought to himself, *how could God curse the man of such bad luck of evil demonic witch?* True to her words, the demonic witch lied to the police about the man, and he was arrested for a crime he had no part in. The man was locked up by Elm's policemen and was imprisoned with other cellmates, one of whom was the clown who had tormented him consistently over the past.

He recalled those days vividly because he would be returning home from working a night shift with a neighbor who was staunchly racist and loathed black people much like the man. The man had to face severe discrimination in that neighborhood and was denied basic rights like owning a home; if that wasn't enough, the clown added to his torments.

The man was processed at the Elms County Correctional Facility jail. Wrongly accused, the man craved vengeance. His innocence had been so corrupted by his thirst to get revenge that one night, four demons from Hell's Gate decided to grant the man demonic powers, demon claws that could slash your skin like butter. The man was delighted, and his thirst for revenge contorted into something even more evil as his claws morphed dangerously more than he could handle.

The demons had given the man so much power that they failed to realize the man was a believer in God and the lord Jesus Christ. Conflicted between the two extremes manifesting inside him, the man became more dangerous than ever. His skin turned green, his red eyes held the cold lust for murder, and blood pooled inside his mouth, his tongue tingling for the taste of vengeance, which could only be satiated when he would feed on the evil doings of people that he came across.

His name was UNKNOWN.

That night, UNKNOWN awakened to something much more than a dream of fear. He felt inhuman power surging through himself. Although he felt he should resist these dark urges wanting him to do evil things, he could not disobey. There was a certain satisfaction and thrill in the power that had taken over him. Not wanting His believer to go astray, God and the lord Jesus Christ offered the man a chance for redemption, but he refused to listen. This began UNKNOWN's spree to get his much-due vengeance.

His first target happened to be a man in a dark alley abusing a woman. UNKNOWN could feel the anger as his claws grew very sharp. Then, without a second delay, he approached the man, ripped his throat out, and fed on it. The woman watched in shock, unable to comprehend what just happened. She didn't know if she was supposed to be grateful to UNKNOWN or run for her life. She chose the latter as fear took over her.

UNKNOWN wasn't like other villains; he was unique and more powerful than any other villain, but what set him apart was that he never fed on the innocent. The people in the city started to figure out UNKNOWN's pattern of murder, but that did not limit his victims.

On a stormy night, a gang of men inside a corner store were eyeing a middle-aged woman purchasing groceries for her family at home. The three gang members follow her 5 miles away from her house in an attempt to rob her. UNKNOWN appeared out of nowhere, tearing apart all three gang members to pieces, feeding on their evil intentions to torture a woman who was working hard to support her family and herself.

The next morning, UNKNOWN was an ordinary working guy who believed in doing the right things; he believed he was using his powers to get vengeance for all the evil in this world. UNKNOWN was a villainous hero because he never harmed the innocent, but his twisted perspective of his powers led him astray. After all, how good could powers from demons be? Only God, the Lord Jesus Christ, knew what darkness lurked in UNKNOWN and that his killings were in no circumstances justified because he didn't obey God's words.

A woman and her son were in the movie theater when the woman began beating her son for eating up all the popcorn. UNKNOWN heard everything from a tall government building. The woman was dragging and abusing her son until one thing led to another, and the Slasher (UNKNOWN) came out of nowhere, taunting the woman. He warned her not to do that again by cutting her hand and tasting her blood. The woman started crying, indicating hurt, disappointment, or sadness.

Although he let her go, UNKNOWN knew better; when it comes to narcissists, tears are just a trick to manipulate and accomplish so much more. Crying is not a difficult thing for narcissists; it is something they can do with a snap of their fingers; they are like actors and actresses who have perfected their craft. However, they lose the desired effect when you know what they are about or their tears mean. Narcissists know it is very important to display some sort of empathy. Many have learned to do just that to convince people that they care about others. Deception is the name of the game.

If the Narcissist can deceive you into thinking that they are empathetic, caring individuals, then you are more likely to trust them or see them as a good person. So beware because a Narcissist will only cry to win your heart so that they can later break your heart. This is a result of their need to be in control of everyone and everything, which is not possible, and therefore, they become disappointed and frustrated. They shed a few tears over their own misfortune or unfulfilled plans. This is the only time their tears come from a genuine place, but these tears are not for anyone else but themselves.

Narcissists cannot handle disappointments. They cannot cope with losing control or facing the reality that they are not in control, which makes them truly sad. They are distraught when they don't get what they want or things don't play out how they want them to. With their tears, they hope to gain pity and sympathy and get someone to help them. A narcissist's tears are only genuine when they are crying over their own losses.

And then...

49 Strangest Unsolved Mysteries

1.   The Body on Somerton Beach

In December 1948, a body was found on Somerton Beach in Adelaide, Australia. The body was a man who was dressed impeccably in a suit with polished shoes, and his head was slumped against a wall. Authorities thought the cause of death was heart failure or, more likely, poisoning, but no trace of poison was found in the autopsy. There wasn't a wallet or identification on the man, and all the tags from his clothing were cut out. The fingerprints that the authorities took of him were also unidentifiable. They even put a photo of the body in the newspapers, and still, no one could identify who the man was. Four months later, after the body was found, detectives found a hidden pocket that was sewn on the inside of his trousers. Inside the pocket was a rolled-up paper from a rare book called the Rubáiyát. The piece of paper had the words "Tamám Shud" on it, meaning "it has ended." After months of looking for the exact book, authorities decide to bury the Somerton Man without identification. Although a cast was taken of the bust, he was embalmed to preserve him. Eight months later, a man walked into the police station. He claimed that just after the body was found, he found a copy of the Rubáiyát in the back of his car that he kept parked near Somerton Beach. He thought nothing of it until he read about the search in a newspaper article. Sure enough, the book had a part of the final page that was torn and matched the piece of paper found in the Somerton Man's trousers. Inside the book was a phone number and some sort of strange code. The phone number led the authorities to a woman named Jessica Thompson, who lived nearby. During her interview, she was very evasive and even claimed she would faint when she saw the bust of the Somerton Man but denied knowing him. However, she said she did sell the book to a man named Alfred Boxall. Unfortunately, Alfred Boxall was still alive and had the copy of the Rubaiyát that Jessica had sold him. The code that was found ended up being even more unhelpful, and as of today, it has still yet to be cracked.

2. The Strange Disappearance of D.B. Cooper

On Wednesday, November 24, 1971, a man identified as Daniel Cooper bought a $20 one-way ticket on Northwest Airlines, Flight 305 from Portland, Oregon to

Seattle, Washington. Cooper was described as in his mid-40s, wearing a business suit, an overcoat, brown shoes, a white shirt, and a black tie. He also carried a briefcase and a brown paper bag. Before the flight took off, he ordered a bourbon and soda from a flight attendant. After the plane was airborne, Cooper handed the flight attendant a note. At first, she just put it in her pocket without looking at it, but then Cooper told her, "Miss, you better look at that note. I have a bomb." Cooper then told her the bomb was in his briefcase and asked her to sit next to him. He opened the briefcase to reveal red-colored sticks surrounded by wires. Cooper told the flight attendant to write down everything he said and then take it to the Captain. The note said, "I want $200,000 by 5 p.m. in cash, exclusively in $20 bills, put in a knapsack. I want two back parachutes and two front parachutes. When we land, I want a fuel truck ready to refuel. No funny stuff, or I'll do the job." FBI agents assembled the ransom money from several Seattle-area banks. Seattle police obtained the parachutes from a local skydiving school.

When Cooper claimed his demands were met, he allowed all passengers and some of the crew to exit the airplane. Cooper told the remaining crew to refuel the plane and chart a course for Mexico City while staying below 10,000 feet. During the flight, Cooper put on a pair of dark wraparound sunglasses, which would make it into the official sketch and become famous to anyone investigating the case. A little after 8 p.m. and somewhere between Seattle and Reno, Nevada, Cooper jumped out of the plane's rear door with two parachutes and the money. He was never seen again. Despite an expansive manhunt and over 45 years of searching, no conclusions have been made as to the man's identity or his fate after he jumped. It is one of the greatest cold cases in FBI and US history.

3. The Black Dahlia Murder

On January 15, 1947, the remains of 22-year-old Elizabeth Short, AKA "The Black Dahlia," were found on the block of 3800 S Norton Avenue in Los Angeles. The body was cut in half and so pale and drained of blood that the woman who found the body mistook it for a mannequin at first. The body was cut with surgical precision, leaving no trauma to internal organs and bones. Her face was also cut from her mouth to ears, leaving an eerie permanent smile. There was no blood on the ground, making it believed that the body was moved after she had been murdered. Nine days after she was discovered, an envelope was sent to the examiner addressed using individual cut-and-paste letters from magazines and newspapers. It read, "The Los Angeles Examiner and other Los Angeles papers, here are Dahlia's belongings and a letter to follow." As promised, the envelope contained Short's Social Security card, birth certificate, photographs, names written on pieces of paper, and an address book with pages missing and the name Mark Hansen embossed on the cover. Gasoline was used to clean the objects, removing the fingerprints. On March 14, a suicide note scrawled in pencil on a bit of paper was found tucked in a shoe in a pile of men's clothing by the ocean's edge at the foot of Breeze Avenue in Venice. The note read:

"To whom it may concern,

I have waited for the police to capture me for the Black Dahlia killing, but they have not. I am too cowardly to turn myself in, so this is the best way out for me. I couldn't help myself for that or this.

Sorry, Mary."

The beach caretaker first saw the pile of clothing and reported the discovery to the lifeguard captain, John Dillon. Dillon immediately notified the West Los Angeles Police Station. The clothes included a coat and trousers of blue herringbone tweed, a brown and white shirt, white jockey shorts, tan socks, and tan moccasin shoes, about size eight. However, the clothes gave no clue about their owner's identity. Although many suspects were named, no authorities were able to identify the Black Dahlia's killer, and the mystery has gone unsolved for over 70 years.

4. Wall Street Bombing of 1920

During the lunch rush on Wall Street in September 1920, a non-descript man driving a cart pressed an old horse forward in front of the US Assay Office, across from the 3. P. Morgan building. He stopped his cart, got down, and immediately disappeared into the crowd. Minutes later, the cart exploded into a hail of metal fragments, immediately killing more than 30 people and injuring 300. The aftermath was horrific, and the death toll rose as the day wore on and more victims succumbed to their injuries. In the beginning, it wasn't obvious that the explosion was an intentional act of terrorism; it was viewed as simply an accident. Maintenance crews cleaned up the damage overnight, throwing away any physical evidence crucial to identifying the perpetrator. By the next morning, Wall Street was back in business. Conspiracy theories were abundant, but the New York Police and Fire Departments, the Bureau of Investigation (the FBI's predecessor), and the US Secret Service were on the job to find the truth. Each lead was actively pursued, and the Bureau interviewed hundreds of people who had been around that area before, during, and after the attack but collected very little information. The few recollections of the driver and wagon were vague and useless. The NYPD was able to reconstruct the bomb and its fuse mechanism, but there was much debate about the nature of the explosive.

However, the most promising lead had come before the explosion. A mailman had found four crudely spelled and printed flyers in the Wall Street area from a group calling itself the "American Anarchist Fighters" that demanded the release of political prisoners. The letters seemed similar to ones used the previous year in two bombing campaigns led by Italian Anarchists. The Bureau investigated up and down the East Coast to trace the printing of these flyers, but they were unsuccessful. Based on bomb attacks over the previous decade, the Bureau initially suspected followers of the Italian Anarchist Luigi Galleani had committed the crime. But the case couldn't be proved, and Galleani had already fled the country. Over the next three years, hot leads turned cold, and promising trails became dead ends. In the end, the bombers were not identified.

5. The Disturbing Death of Elisa Lam

On January 26, 2013, 21-year-old Canadian tourist Elisa Lam checked into the Cecil Hotel in downtown Los Angeles. When she never checked out on February 1 nor had any contact with her parents, the Los Angeles Police Department was contacted. On February 19, 18 days from the last time she was seen, Lam's body was found floating and naked in a water tank on the roof of the Cecil Hotel. Her body was found due to hotel guests complaining about the hotel's water pressure. One couple even reported that the water was coming out black and had a bad taste. According to the hotel's manager, when Lam first checked in, she was staying in a hostel-style room with other travelers, but she was later moved to her own private room due to complaints from her roommates about odd behavior. She was last seen on surveillance footage in the hotel's elevator. The footage showed Lam acting strange and peculiar, almost like she was hiding. She also moved her hands in strange ways, and it looked like she was talking to someone who was out of the security camera's view. After her body and the surveillance footage were found, it was suggested she was on some sort of hallucinogenic drug. Even though Lam took four different medications for her bipolar disorder, toxicology studies reported that there were no traces of any drugs or alcohol that could have contributed to her death. There was also a theory that she was murdered and died as a result of drowning, but the autopsy report showed no evidence of trauma. No one knows how she could access the roof or climb into the water tank and shut the 20-pound lid by herself.

6. Jack the Ripper

In 1888, in the foggy dark streets of the East End of London, better known as the Whitechapel District, lived a serial killer that would go down in history as Jack the Ripper. Even though the Whitechapel District was known for its violence and crime, the string of murders conducted by Jack the Ripper would terrorize the public like no one had seen before. He was described as a madman with no clear motive. Even though his most famous murders only included five women (known as "The Canonical Five"), many theories suggest that he claimed the lives of up to 11 women. All of the victims of the Canonical Five were prostitutes, as it was common for women who lived in the Whitechapel District to take on as a means to survive. All five killings took place within a mile of each other from August 7 to September 10, 1888. Several other murders occurring around that period have also been investigated as the work of "Leather Apron" (another nickname given to the murderer). Some letters were allegedly sent by the killer to the London Metropolitan Police Service (often known as Scotland Yard), taunting officers about his gruesome activities and speculating on murders to come. The name "Jack the Rippe" originates from a letter (which is famously known now as the "From Hell" letter) that was published at the time of the attacks. Despite countless investigations claiming definitive evidence of the brutal killer's identity, their true name and motive are still unknown.

7. The Zodiac Killer

In the late 1960s and early 1970s, a serial killer known as "The Zodiac Killer" terrorized Northern California. There were at least five victims, but later on, the murderer would claim he killed at least 37 people in total. On December 20, 1968, on Lake Herman Road in Vallejo, 17-year-old David Faraday and 16-year-old Betty Lou Jensen were shot and killed while sitting in a parked car in a gravel parking area. By the time police arrived, Betty was found dead, but David was still alive. Unfortunately, he died on the way to the hospital. This was the first murder that the Zodiac Killer conducted and got away with. The Zodiac's next crime would happen on July 4, 1969, in Blue Rock Springs Park, only a few minutes from the previous crime. The Zodiac Killer approached a parked car with a flashlight and then murdered 22-year-old Darlene Ferrin and 19-year-old Michael Mageau. Both were still alive when found, but only Mageau would survive. He could describe the shooter as a young, white male, 26-30 years old, with a stocky build, 200 pounds or larger, about 5'8, with light brown curly hair and a large face. Within an hour, the police received a phone call from someone who claimed to be the shooter and the shooter in the Lake Herman Road murders. On August 1, 1969, the San Francisco Chronicle, the San Francisco Examiner, and the Vallejo Herald received a handwritten letter from someone who claimed to be the shooter. The letters revealed specific details about the killings to prove that the writer was indeed the murderer. All the letters were signed with a circle with a cross through it, the symbol that would eventually be known as the mark of the Zodiac Killer. Also included in the letter were three different codes that the Zodiac Killer demanded to be printed in newspapers or else he would kill again. The

Zodiac Killer said that the cracked codes would reveal his identity.

On August 4, 1969, another letter was received that started with the phrase saying, "This is the Zodiac speaking," marking the first time the killer referred to himself as the Zodiac. On August 8, the code was cracked by a couple in Salinas, California. The codes read: "I like killing because it is so much fun. It is more fun than killing wild game in the forest because man is the most dangerous animal of all to kill. Something gives me the most thrilling experience; it is even better than getting your rocks off with a girl. The best part of it is that when I die, I will be reborn in paradise, and those I have killed will become my slaves. I will not give you my name because you will slow down or stop my slave collection for the afterlife." After claiming three more lives and causing nationwide terror, the Zodiac Killer wrote his final letter on January 29, 1974, concluding the letter with a new score, "Me–37 SFPD=0." The true identity of the killer has never been found.

8. The Case of JonBenét Ramsey

On December 26, 1996, in Boulder, Colorado, Patsy Ramsey claimed to have discovered a ransom note for her

6-year-old daughter JonBenét Ramsey on the back staircase inside the Ramsey home. This prompted her to call the police at 5:52 a.m. to report JonBenét missing. The only people inside the house were John Ramsey, her father, Patsy, her mother, and her brother Burke. Oddly enough, JonBenét's body was found inside the home in the utility room in the basement less than eight hours later. The body was found by John, and duct tape was found across her mouth and a smooth cord around her neck. When police arrived, it was suspected that the crime scene was heavily compromised due to multiple people arriving at the scene. The police had also claimed they had not searched the house after Patsy's initial call because there was no reason to believe JonBenet was in the house. At the time of her death, JonBenét was known as a child beauty queen superstar, having won at least five high-end child beauty competitions. Her death was ultimately ruled a homicide. The autopsy stated that JonBenét's official cause of death was "asphyxia by strangulation associated with craniocerebral trauma." Due to JonBenét's beauty queen popularity and her mother being a former beauty queen, the case caused nationwide and media interest. Today, the crime is still unsolved and remains an open investigation with the Boulder Police Department.

9. Chicago Tylenol Murders

On September 29, 1982, seven people in the Chicago area ingested poisoned Tylenol pills, consequently collapsing and dying shortly after. The victims included 12-year-old Mary Kellerman, 27-year-old Mary Reiner, 31-year-old Mary McFarland, 35-year-old Paula Prince, 27-year-old Adam Janus, 25-year-old Stanley Janus, and 19-year-old Theresa Janus. Adam Janus ingested a Tylenol and died at the hospital. When the family came back to mourn, Stanley Janus and his wife Theresa took a Tylenol and died, making it three deaths in the same family on the same day. However, this tragedy is what led investigators to connect the dots. Cook County investigator Nick Pishos compared the Janus Tylenol bottle to Mary Kellerman's and noticed one similarity: a control number: MC2880. Deputy medical examiner Edmund Donoghue asked Pishos to smell the bottles, and Pishos replied that they both smelled like almonds. The poison cyanide is known to smell like bitter almonds, which, in large amounts, can cause seizures, cardiac arrest, and respiratory failure. The blood tests on all of the victims showed that they had taken a dose 100–1000 times the lethal amount. Donoghue spoke to an attorney from Johnson & Johnson, Tylenol's parent company, and after all the victims were buried on October 1, 1982, that the Tylenol bottles were intentionally poisoned with potassium cyanide. Immediately, the manufacturer recalled over 31 million bottles of Tylenol, and warnings were issued. They also offered to replace recalled bottles with new bottles. They offered a $100,000 reward to anyone with any information on the perpetrator. These precautions cost the company over $100,000,000. There were several more copycat deaths across the United States after the initial incident had occurred. This led to the invention of safety seals on medicine bottles today. To this day, no suspect has ever been charged or convicted of the poisonings.

10. The Unsolved Hinterkaifeck Murders

On the evening of March 31, 1922, on Hinterkaifeck Farm in Bavaria, Germany, six residents were murdered with a pickaxe. The victims included husband and wife Andreas and Cäzilia Gruber, their widowed daughter Viktoria Gabriel, Viktoria's children, Cäzilia and Josef, and the family's maid Maria Baumgartner. Two-year-old Josef was killed in his crib, and Maria was killed in her bed while the rest of the family was then murdered in the barn and stacked on top of each other. Upon the discovery, authorities concluded that the murderer actually lived on the farm for six days after they committed the crime. Even after the family had died, cattle were still being fed, meals were being eaten in the kitchen, neighbors reported seeing smoke rising from the chimney, and the family dog was tied up to a post when the mailman came on Saturday. The bodies were discovered the next day. What makes this crime even more chilling is that Maria was actually hired the same day she was killed, replacing the previous maid who had quit six months earlier due to the house "being haunted." She reported hearing footsteps and voices in the attic of the family. Around the time the previous maid had quit, the Gruber family had also begun to hear voices from the attic. Andreas had also noticed a set of house keys had gone missing, an unfamiliar newspaper in the house that he had never seen before, plus scratches on the family's tool shed like someone had tried to pick the lock. He had also reported seeing a pair of unfamiliar footsteps leading from the woods toward the back entrance of the family's home. Despite repeated arrests, no murderer has ever been found. The files were closed in 1955, and the house was demolished.

11. The Ghost Ship of the Mary Celeste

On December 4, 1872, a British-American ship called The Mary Celeste was found abandoned and floating in the Atlantic Ocean. It was found to be perfectly seaworthy and with its cargo fully intact, except for a lifeboat, which appeared to have been boarded in an orderly fashion. But why? We may never know because no one on board was ever heard from again. The Mary Celeste set sail from New York bound for Genoa, Italy, in November 1872. The ship was manned by Captain Benjamin Briggs and seven crew members, including Briggs' wife and their 2-year-old daughter. Supplies on board were set to last for six months, and there were luxurious items on board, including a sewing machine and an upright piano. Historians and commentators generally agree that some extraordinary and alarming circumstances must have arisen to abandon such a worthy ship. However, the last entry on the ship's daily log reveals nothing unusual. Inside the ship, all appeared to be in order. Conspiracy theories over the years have included mutiny, pirate attacks, and even a giant octopus or sea monster attack. However, the cause behind this ghost ship remains unsolved.

12. The Watcher House

In June 2014, Maria, Derek Broaddus, and their three young children were getting ready to move into their new home, 657 Boulevard in Westfield, New Jersey. They claimed the 6-bedroom house was their "dream home" and located just a couple of blocks away from Maria's childhood home in one of the top 30th safest cities in the United States. Three days after closing the sale, a letter arrived in their new mailbox before the Broaddus family had even begun to move in. The letter was addressed to "The New Owner" in big clunky handwriting. The typed letter read as follows:

"Dearest new neighbor at 657 Boulevard, allow me to welcome you to the neighborhood. How did you end up here? Did 657 Boulevard call to you with its force within? 657 Boulevard has been the subject of my family for decades now, and as it approaches its 110th birthday, I have been put in charge of watching and waiting for its second coming. My grandfather and my father watched the house in the 1920s and the 1960s. It is now my time. Who am I? There are hundreds and hundreds of cars

that drive by 657 Boulevard each day. Maybe I am in one. Look at all the windows you can see from 657 Boulevard. Maybe I am in one. Look out at any of the many windows in 657 Boulevard at everyone who strolls by each day. Maybe I am one." The letter also mentioned specifics about the Broaddus family. *"You have children. I have seen them,"* the letter continued, *"So far, I think there are three that I have counted. Do you need to fill the house with the young blood I requested? Better for me. Was your old house too small for the growing family? Or was it greed to bring me your children? Once I know their names, I will call them and draw them to me."* At the bottom of the letter, the author used a cursive font to sign *"The Watcher."*

After receiving the letter, the Broaddus family reached out to the previous family, John and Andrea Woods, who had sold them the house. They stated that during the 23 years of living at 657 Boulevard, they had never received a letter like that except once a few days before they were getting ready to move out of the house. The Woods family also stated they had never felt watched in the two decades they had lived at the house and, in fact, rarely felt the need to lock their door at night. While they thought the note they received was odd, they threw it away without concern. Still, the two families went to the police with the letter, and an investigation was opened. The police warned the families not to tell anyone about the letters, including their neighbors, who were now all suspects. Two weeks later, even though the Broaddus family still hadn't moved in, they received a second letter with even more chilling specifics about the family, including the children's birth order and nicknames. The Watcher also asked, "Will the children sleep in the attic? Or will you all sleep on the second floor? Who has the bedrooms facing the street? I will know as soon as you move in. It will help me to know who is in which bedroom. Then, I can plan better." Several weeks later, the Broaddus family had put their plans on hold to move in, and a third letter arrived saying, "Where have you gone to? 657 Boulevard is missing you." By the end of 2014, the case had stalled. There was no digital trail, and the mental effects were taking a toll on the Broaddus family. There were no fingerprints or way to place somebody at the crime scene. Only six months after they received the letters, they decided to sell the home. 657 Boulevard has been sold and is currently off the market, while The Watcher's identity remains a mystery.

13. The Mystery of the Circleville Letters

In 1976, residents of Circleville, Ohio, began receiving threatening mail that has haunted them ever since. The letters were from Columbus but had no return address. They accused school bus driver Mary Gillespie and the school superintendent of having an extramarital affair. One of the letters was even addressed to Mary's husband, Ron, who threatened his life if he didn't put a stop to the affair. In 1977, Ron died in a suspicious one-car crash that involved gunshots. However, when the Sheriff ruled the death an accident, other residents of Circleville began receiving letters accusing the Sheriff of covering up the so-called "accident." Ron's sister's husband, Paul Freshour, was convicted of writing the letters after there was an attempt to murder Mary via a booby-trap-rigged pistol. Even after he was thrown behind bars, the Circleville Letters continued throughout the 1970s and the early 1980s. Freshour even received one in prison. In 1994, Freshour was released, and he claimed his innocence until his death in 2012. The true identity of the Circleville Letter Writer remains unknown.

Related: The True Meaning of Your True Crime Obsession

14. The Sodder Children Disappearance

On the night before Christmas in 1945 in Fayetteville, West Virginia, George and Jennie Sodder were asleep with nine of their children when a fire started around 1:00 in the morning. George, Jennie, and four of their children managed to escape. The remaining children, 14-year-old Maurice, 12-year-old Martha, 9-year-old Louis, 8-year-old Jennie, and 5-year-old Betty, remained in the house. Between the five of them, they shared two bedrooms located upstairs. George broke into the house to save the rest of the children, but the staircase was on fire. When he went outside to retrieve his ladder, it was missing from its normal spot. Plus, both of his coal trucks, which he was going to use to stand on top of, were strangely not starting.

Marion, one of the children who escaped the fire, ran to a neighbor's house to phone the fire department, but the operator didn't pick up. When another neighbor called, the operator failed to pick up the phone again. That same neighbor actually drove to town and found the fire chief, FJ Morris, in person and told him about the fire. However, even though the fire station was located a mere 2.5 miles away from the house, the firefighters didn't reach the Sodder home until 8 a.m., seven hours after the fire began.

When they got there, the house was literally burnt to ash. Authorities sifted through the ash to try and find the remains of the missing 5 children, but nothing was found, and they were presumed dead due to the fire. Morris suggested that the fire was so hot that it literally cremated the children's bodies, including their bones. While that theory sounds reasonable, it's not entirely accurate because bones are typically left behind even when flesh is burned away.

Additionally, there was no smell of burning flesh reported during or after the fire. The cause of the fire was deemed to be bad wiring, and the five missing children were issued death certificates. Soon after the fire, George and Jennie began to suspect that their children were not dead but instead kidnapped, and the fire was deliberately set as a diversion. In fact, George had the wiring checked earlier that fall by the power company, which had deemed the wiring in safe working order. While the fire was in progress, a woman came forward and said she saw all of the five missing children peering from a passing car. Another woman staying at a Charleston hotel had seen the children's photos in a newspaper and said she had seen four of the five a week after the fire. "The children were accompanied by two women and two men, all of Italian dissent," she said in a statement. "I tried to talk to the children in a friendly manner, but the men appeared hostile and wouldn't allow it."

From the 1950s until Jennie Sodder's death in the late 1980s, the Sodder family maintained a billboard on State Route 16 with pictures of the five vanished children and offered a reward for information. The last known surviving Sodder child, Sylvia, still doesn't believe her siblings perished in the fire. To this day, they have never been found.

Related: The Sordid and Grisly True Story of Jeffrey Dahmer

15. The Axeman of New Orleans

Starting in 1918 and over a period of 18 months, the city of New Orleans was haunted by a serial killer known as "The Axeman." The Axeman was the personification of the boogeyman, only attacking at night, and was rumored to be responsible for 12 attacks and six deaths. To make this mystery even more chilling, he seemed to only creep on his victims while they slept. Oddly enough, The Axeman never used his own tools and only used what he could find in the victim's house, usually an ax, which he would then leave at the crime scene. The majority of the Axeman's victims were Italian immigrants or Italian-Americans, leading many citizens of New Orleans to believe that the crimes were ethnically motivated. Many media outlets drew frenzy from this aspect of the crimes, even suggesting Mafia involvement despite the pure lack of evidence. Other crime analysts have suggested that the Axeman killings were related to sex and that the murderer was perhaps a sadist specifically seeking female victims. Other theories include that the Axeman killed male victims only when they blocked his attempts to murder women, supported by cases in which the woman of a household was murdered but not the man. A less likely theory is that the serial killer committed the murders in an attempt to promote jazz music, as suggested by a letter that the murderer himself was rumored to have written, which stated that he would spare the lives of those who played jazz in their homes. The Axeman was never identified, and the murders remain unsolved.

16. The Death of the Boy in the Box

On February 25, 1957, the body of an unidentified boy was found in a box in an illegal dumping ground near Philadelphia. The boy was estimated to be around four to six years old, weighed about 30 pounds, and stood around 3'3". He was found naked but wrapped in a blanket. His hair was recently cut, and his body was recently washed clean. There were small scars on his chin, groin, and left ankle, some of which proved he went through a small medical procedure. He was found with blunt force trauma to the head that was determined to be the cause of death, and there were no witnesses. The body was found by a young man who was walking through the abandoned lot. Strangely, the man waited a whole day before contacting the police, and even a second man had previously found the boy's body but had not contacted the police because he didn't want to get involved. With the cold weather and delayed phone calls, police weren't able to accurately estimate the time of the boy's death. In order to identify the boy, the body was kept in the morgue while visitors from 19 different states tried to look for identifiable marks to no avail. Police sent out 400,000 flyers of the boy to police stations, post offices, and courthouses nationwide.

Even the American Medical Association described the boy, but it led nowhere. The police compared the boy's footprints to hospitals in the area and even took fingerprints, but no records showed that the boy ever existed. In 2016, the National Center for Missing & Exploited Children released a forensic facial reconstruction of the victim and added him to their database. Unfortunately, the boy has never been identified, and the case still remains open.

17. The Mysterious Drowning of Natalie Wood, Robert Wagner and Natalie Wood

On November 29, 1981, around 7:30 a.m., actress Natalie Wood's body was found floating face down in the Pacific Ocean about 200 yards away from Catalina Island's Blue Cavern Point. She was wearing only a flannel nightgown, blue wool socks, and a red down jacket. Wood was one of Hollywood's biggest stars until her death, with roles that included Miracle on 34th Street and West Side Story. Eerily, Wood's mother had given the fear of dark water to her daughter because a fortune teller had prophesied that she would die of drowning. As a child, it was reported that her fear of water was so great she was even afraid to wash her hair and had recurring nightmares about drowning.

Wood and actor Christopher Walken had been working on the film Brainstorm then. She invited Walken to join her and her husband, Robert Wagner, on their yacht, the Splendor. According to the captain and family friend Dennis Davern, Wood became infatuated with Walken during filming. Wagner had flown to the movie set to "make sure [he] wasn't making a fool of [himself] over this." The group left on the boat around the afternoon of November 27, 1981. Everyone on the boat, including the Captain, had been drinking for much of the weekend. On that Friday night, Wood and Wagner had argued to the point where Davern became concerned and asked Walken to get involved. Walken refused to intervene and is quoted saying, "Never get involved in an argument between a man and his wife." Davern ended up taking Wood to shore that night using the ship's dinghy, The Prince Valiant, and they slept at a hotel in Avalon.

They returned to the yacht the next morning, and Wood agreed to spend the rest of the weekend onboard. That afternoon, Wood and Walken went to shore to begin drinking at Doug's Harbor Reef and Saloon. They had much to drink, and their waitress reported Wood not eating much of her dinner and stumbling out of the restaurant when they were done. Walken and Wood boarded the dinghy and returned to the yacht around 10 p.m. A witness from the Harbor Patrol said they heard Wood scream about something, but they brushed it off because she was intoxicated. Witnesses from a nearby boat claimed they heard shouts around midnight. However, a party was going on nearby, so they thought it was from the party and didn't intervene. One of the witnesses, John Payne, said he heard a woman scream, "Help me! Someone help me!" coming from the stern of the Splendor and potentially from a dinghy. He then thought he heard a man's voice say, "Okay, honey, we'll get you," but the tone was mocking, which is why he thought the cries were associated with the party.

According to Wagner, a non-violent argument broke out between him and Walken over politics. Wood wasn't involved, quickly became bored, and assumedly went to bed. However, Wagner didn't realize she was missing until he went to kiss her goodnight around 1:30 a.m. The Coast Guard was alerted, and Wood was found floating six hours later, about a mile away from the yacht, with the dinghy not too far from her. Los Angeles County coroner Thomas

Noguchi ruled the cause of her death to be accidental drowning and hypothermia. According to Noguchi, Wood had been drinking, and she may have slipped while trying to re-board the dinghy. Wood's sister Lana expressed doubts, alleging that she could not swim, had been terrified of water all her life, and would never have left the yacht on her own by dinghy. To this day, her death remains a mystery.

18. The Keddie Cabin Murders

On April 12, 1981, in Keddie, California, the Sharp family and some friends slept inside Cabin 28 at the Keddie Resort Lodge. Sheila Sharp would wake up to find her mother, Sue, her brother, Johnny, and their family friend, Dana Wingate, brutally murdered inside the cabin while her 12-year-old sister, Tina, was missing from the scene. Sheila only escaped the murders by sleeping at a friend's cabin next door.

Surprisingly, they found Sheila's two younger brothers, Greg and Rick, and their friend Justin Smartt, asleep and safe in another bedroom inside Cabin 28. Tina's remains would be found by an anonymous tip on the third anniversary of the murders. Her skull was found 50 miles away from Keddie in a different county. There were only two suspects that the police examined: Marty Smartt and his roommate, Bo Boubede. Marty Smartt was married to Marilyn Smartt, and they were parents to Justin Smartt. Marty was apparently an abusive husband. Since Sheila Sharp had just escaped an abusive relationship herself, there were reports that she was giving Marilyn some counseling.

When Marty found out that Sheila was interfering in his marriage, he reportedly "went ballistic." Soon after the murders, Marty left Keddie for Reno, Nevada. Law enforcement felt that the murders took more than one person to conduct, which is why they took Boubede into questioning as an accomplice. Boubede was also an ex-con. Despite so much more to the case, the investigation oddly stopped there. There was evidence that seemingly went unnoticed and people of interest that were not examined properly. The murderer of the Keddie crime has not been identified, and the case remains unsolved.

Related: Inside Lori Vallow Daybell's Life Today

19. The Gardner Museum Heist

On March 18, 1990, the Isabella Stewart Gardner Museum in Boston fell victim to one of the greatest art thefts in history. Only 13 pieces of art were stolen, but the combined value of all those paintings was worth over $500 million. On the night of the heist, two inexperienced guards were on duty. One of them was Richard E. Abath, who was a music school dropout and part of a rock band. On his own admission, he confessed that he would come to work drunk or stoned after a performance. Still, he insisted he was sober the night of the robbery.

At 12:54 a.m., a fire alarm went off on the museum's third floor. When Abath went to investigate, there was no fire. Whether this was part of the thieves' scheme is unknown. At 1:24 a.m., two men dressed as Boston Police buzzed the security desk where Abath was stationed. The men said they were responding to a disturbance call and demanded entry. St. Patrick's Day parties were happening around the city, so the disturbance call made sense to Abath.

The guard buzzed the men into the employee entrance, which violated museum protocol. Then, when the men reached Abath behind the desk, one of them said, "You look familiar. I think we have a default warrant out for you.

Come out here and show us some identification." Abath was tricked into leaving his control desk, which had the only button to trigger a silent alarm. He was then instructed to face the wall and was handcuffed. The second guard then appeared, and he was also "arrested."

When the second guard asked why he was being arrested, one of the men replied, "You're not being arrested. This is a robbery. Don't give us any problems; you won't get hurt." An hour and 21 minutes later, the thieves made out with 13 timeless works of art. They cut Rembrandt's Christ in the Storm on the Sea of Galilee and A Lady and Gentleman in Black from their frames; removed Vermeer's The Concert and Flinck's Landscape with an Obelisk from their frames; pulled an ancient Chinese bronze Gu (or beaker), from a table; and took a small self-portrait etching by Rembrandt from the side of a chest. In the museum today, empty frames now stand where the paintings were hung as a remembrance. The thieves have yet to be caught, and the location of the art pieces is still unknown. The Isabella Stewart Gardner Museum has set a $10 million reward for information leading to the recovery of the stolen works.

20. The Disappearance of Jimmy Hoffa in 1966

Bettmann via Getty Images James Riddle "Jimmy" Hoffa was the former Teamsters president from 1958 to 1971. The Teamsters were known primarily as a labor union for drivers. At just age 18, Hoffa succeeded in getting dock workers better pay by organizing a strike. He began organizing for the Teamsters a year later and gradually rose through the ranks. Hoffa's influence as the Teamsters president was significant. At the time, 90% of US transportation was controlled by Teamsters, who were controlled by Hoffa.

In 1941, Hoffa and his Teamsters were in a turf battle with their rivals in Detroit. It was during this time that Hoffa got involved with the Mob. Hoffa hired the Mob to get rid of the rivals in the city. Although it worked, Hoffa was essentially owned by the Mafia. The Mob and Hoffa had a symbiotic relationship in which the Mob was able to take loans out of the Teamsters' pension fund. These funds funneled into many Las Vegas casinos, and, in return, Hoffa and the pension fund got a favorable return on these loans.

Despite his connections to the Mob, Hoffa was still loved by the Teamsters as he was known for increasing benefits and wages for workers. Throughout the 1940s and 1950s, Hoffa was able to have good relations with the Mob until he started a 13-year prison sentence in 1967 for crimes including bribery, jury tampering, and mail fraud. President Nixon then pardoned him in 1971 as long as he abstained from union involvement until 1980. This would lead to Hoffa's downfall. In July 1976, it was discovered that the Teamsters largest pension fund had been robbed of hundreds of millions of dollars, and only two weeks later, Hoffa vanished.

On July 30, 1975, Hoffa was seen at a Detroit area restaurant, Machus Red Fox. According to notes Hoffa wrote to his family, he was asked to meet two acquaintances at 2 p.m. The acquaintances were suspects, Anthony "Tony Jack" Giacalone and Anthony "Tony Pro" Provenzano, both members of the Mob. However, they never showed up to the meeting, and when they were both questioned by the FBI, they insisted that no meeting had ever been organized. Despite extensive surveillance and bugging by the FBI, investigators found that the Mafia members who they thought were involved were generally unwilling to talk about Hoffa's disappearance, even in private. Despite the lack of evidence, there is wide agreement among crime historians and investigators close to the case that Hoffa was murdered by his enemies in the

Mafia. However, key details of his disappearance remain either unknown or unprovable, and this has ensured that no individuals have ever been charged in relation to the case. Hoffa's body was never found.

Related: 65 Best Movies Based on True Stories

21. The Eight-Day Bride

On May 20, 1947, the body of 22-year-old Christina Kettlewell was found 150 feet away from her honeymoon cottage in just nine inches of water on the banks of a river in Severn Falls, Ontario. Just eight days prior, on May 12, Christina had eloped with 26-year-old war veteran John Ray "Jack" Ketterwell after knowing each other for three years. Jack had a friend named Ronald Barrie, a 28-year-old immigrant from Italy and a professional ballroom dancer. It was reported that Jack, Christina, and Ronald spent an "inordinate amount of time" together. Christina's family even thought that Ronald was in love with Christina. Following the elopement, the newlywed Ketterwells spent the next few days at a rented apartment in Toronto.

Bizarrely, Ronald joined them for the entirety of their honeymoon, and on May 17, the trio headed to Ronald's remote cottage in Severn Falls, which was only accessible by boat. It was reported that Christina began acting strangely during that time. She would cry and, at other times, seemed dazed. Evidence suggests that Christina had conversations with Ronald about whether or not Jack truly loved her.

On May 20, Christina disappeared, and Ronald's cabin mysteriously caught on fire. Ronald returned to the cabin to find a disoriented Jack sitting in the cabin with an apparent head injury and pulled him out of the flames. It was then reported he looked for Christina but couldn't find her anywhere in the cottage. Ronald then said that the cottage burned down in just an hour. He then took Jack into the boat back to the mainland of Severn Falls, took his friend to the hospital, and then contacted the police. It was then that the situation became worse. Later, Christina's body was found by the owner of a boathouse in the area. Her body was free from burns or any signs of violence. An autopsy found traces of codeine in her stomach, but her ultimate cause of death was declared a drowning.

Interestingly enough, Major Lawrence Scardifield, who acted as a first responder to the fire, reported that he saw no signs of Christina's body in the area when he went to get water to help extinguish the flames from the house just hours earlier. Jack, Ronald, and 20 other people were questioned by police. Despite possible theories, including that Christina committed suicide, this case remains unsolved.

Related: The Best True Crime Documentaries

22. The Creepy Murder in Room 1046

On January 22, 1935, a man calling himself Roland T. Owen checked into the Hotel President in Kansas City, Missouri. He showed up with no luggage; he was described as being 20 to 35 years old, had brown hair, a scar on his scalp visible above the ear, and a case of cauliflower ear. He was nicely dressed in a black coat and received the key to room 1846. The maid, Mary Soptic, said Owen allowed her to clean while he was in the room but asked not to lock the door behind her because his friend was about to visit the room very soon. Soptic said he kept the blinds tightly drawn and the lights off except for one dim lamp. Other staff members who entered the room mentioned that same detail. Soptic also mentioned that Owen "was either worried about something or afraid" and "always wanted to kinda keep in the dark."

At 4 p.m., Soptic returned with fresh towels to find Owen lying on the bed, completely dressed, in the dark, with the door unlocked. She also saw a note that read, "Don, I will be back in fifteen minutes. Wait." The next morning, January 3, Soptic returned to clean the room. She noticed that the door had been locked from the outside and assumed Owen had locked it while he was leaving the room.

However, Owen was sitting inside, again with the lights off, which meant that someone else had locked the door from outside the room. When Soptic was cleaning, Owen answered a telephone call and said, "No, Don, I don't want to eat. I am not hungry. I just had breakfast," repeating, "No. I am not hungry."

Soptic arrived later that evening to bring fresh towels and heard two male voices coming from inside the room. When she knocked on the door, she heard a rough voice say, "Who is it?" When she explained that she had fresh towels, the voice replied, "We don't need any." During the night, a woman staying in room 1848 would report hearing loud voices, both male and female, cursing on the same floor; there was a party going on that night in room 1055. The next morning, January 4, around 7 a.m., the hotel switchboard operator noticed that Owen's phone had been off the hook for quite some time without being in use, so she sent the bellboy, Randolph Propst, to see what was up. Despite the door having a "Do Not Disturb" sign, Propst knocked several times and heard a voice that said, "Come in. Turn on the lights."

However, the door was locked, and no one was getting up to let the bellboy in. So, after knocking repeatedly, Propst simply said, "Put the phone back on the hook," assuming that Owen was drunk. About an hour and a half later, at around 8:30 a.m., the phone was still off the hook, and another bellboy, Harold Pike, let himself into the room with a passkey. Using only the light from the hall, Pike discovered Owen lying on the bed naked and assumedly drunk. He also noticed that the bedding was darkened around Owen. The phone stand was kicked down to the ground, so he fixed it and returned it to the receiver.

From 10:30 to 10:45 a.m., the phone was again off the receiver. They sent Propst to resolve the situation, and when he opened the door, he saw a truly horrific scene. Propst told the police, "When I entered the room, this man was within two feet of the door on his knees and elbows, holding his head in his hands. I saw blood on his head. I then turned the light on. I looked around and saw blood on the walls, on the bed, and in the bathroom. This frightened me, and I immediately left the room and went downstairs." Owen had been bound with a cord around his neck, wrists, and ankles. His neck had bruising, suggesting someone had been attempting to strangle him. He had been stabbed more than once in the chest above the heart, and one of the wounds had punctured his lung. Blows to his head had left him with a skull fracture on the right side. In addition to the blood Propst had seen, there was some additional spatter on the ceiling.

Dr. Flanders cut the cords from Owen's wrist and asked him who had done this to him. "Nobody," he answered. When they asked what had caused these injuries, Owen said he had fallen and hit his head on the bathtub. The doctor asked if he had been trying to kill himself. After saying no, Owen lost consciousness and was taken to the hospital. He was completely comatose by the time he arrived and died shortly after midnight on January 5. Although Owen's true identity was revealed a year and a half later as Artemus Ogletree, no suspects have ever been identified. The Kansas City police continue to investigate.

Related: Who Is Jennifer Fairgate From Unsolved Mysteries?

23. The Shark Arm Murders

In early 1935, Coogee Aquarium and Swimming Baths in Sydney, Australia, were floundering. The world was in the middle of the Great Depression, and the aquarium's owner, Bert Hobson, needed something to attract customers. His spirits were lifted when he and his son caught a 14-foot, one-ton tiger shark off the coast and put it in their pool. There had been numerous shark attacks in the area, and Hobson thought it was the perfect thing to save his business.

About a week after catching the shark and in front of crowds of families, the shark began to convulse and vomit, spitting up a rat, a bird, and a human arm. Hobson called the police, and they fished out the arm, which had a tattoo of two boxers fighting, which was located inside the forearm. The shark was killed, and the stomach was cut open to look for any other remains, but none were found. Using new fingerprint technology, they were able to identify the arm's original operator to a 45-year-old Jimmy Smith, who had been missing since April 7, 1935.

Early investigations into Smith's disappearance and shark consumption led police to a Sydney businessman named Reginald William Lloyd Holmes. Holmes was a smuggler who also ran a successful family boat-building business at Lavender Bay, New South Wales. Holmes had employed Smith several times to work insurance scams, including one in 1934 in which an over-insured pleasure cruiser named Pathfinder was sunk. Shortly afterward, the pair began a "partnership" with Patrick Francis Brady, an ex-serviceman and convicted forger. With signatures from Holmes' friends and clients provided by the boat tycoon, Brady would forge checks for small amounts against their bank accounts, which he and Smith then cashed. Police were later able to figure out that Smith had been blackmailing Holmes.

Smith was last seen drinking and playing cards with Patrick Francis Brady at the Cecil Hotel in southern Sydney after telling his wife he was going fishing. Brady had rented a small cottage at the time Smith went missing. Police alleged that Smith was murdered at this cottage. Port Hacking and Gunnamatta Bay were searched by the Australian Navy and the Air Force, but the rest of Smith's body was never found.

Related: On Her Shelf: Crime Junkie Host Ashley Flowers on Her True Crime Book and the Podcasts You Need to Know

24. The Lost Colony of Roanoke

In 1587, English colonial governor John White led a group of people from Britain to found an English colony, settling on Roanoke Island, a chain of barrier islands now known as the Outer Banks near North Carolina. When rations were running low, White left for more supplies. When he returned three years later, he found the colony carefully abandoned, with all houses and military constructions dismantled with care.

Before he had left the colony, White had instructed his people that if they were taken by force, someone was to carve a cross into a nearby tree, but there was no cross nor sign they had been brutally taken over. The only clue was the word "Croatoan," the name of a Native American tribe that allied with the English colonists, which was carved into a post. White took this to mean that the colonists had moved to Croatoan Island. Ongoing investigations have claimed that the colonists had been slaughtered by the Powhatan tribe. Still, there is no archaeological evidence to support this, and a recent re-examination indicates that any massacre that occurred was not of this particular group of colonists but rather a group of colonists who had arrived earlier. More theories involve an amalgamation between the colonists and the Croatians, but so far, no DNA evidence has identified any descendants of the colony.

Related: Dateline NBC Correspondent Dennis Murphy Talks True Crime and More

25. The Disappearance of Dorothy Arnold

Dorothy Harriet Camille Arnold was a wealthy New York socialite, the daughter of perfume importer Francis Rose Arnold, and his wife Mary Martha Parks Arnold. As far as anyone knew, she had a happy home life. On the morning of December 12, 1910, she left her home on the Upper East Side of Manhattan and told her mother that she was headed downtown to buy an evening dress.

According to The New York Times, when her mother asked if she could accompany her daughter, Dorothy said, "No. When I find the gown I want, I will telephone you, and you can come down and see it."

When she left the house, she had over $30 in her pocket. In today's currency, that would be more than $750. On her way down 5th Avenue, she stopped at a grocery store on 59th Street to buy some chocolate, then at a bookstore on 27th Street, where she bought a copy of Engaged Girl Sketches, a humorous collection of short romantic stories.

Around the time when she bought the book, she ran into a friend from college, Gladys King. The two talked about a party they had both been invited to, the same party that Dorothy was buying a dress for. Gladys left to meet her mother for lunch, and Dorothy was never seen again.

Francis Arnold was reluctant to gain publicity over his daughter's disappearance and initially employed the help of private investigators. After unsuccessful attempts, the family filed a missing person report with the New York City Police Department in January 1911. Various theories, sightings, and rumors regarding Arnold's disappearance circulated in the years and decades after she was last seen. Still, the circumstances of her disappearance have never been resolved, and her fate remains unknown.

Related: What Happened to Chris Watts' Girlfriend Nichol Kessinger?

26. The Murder of Bugsy Siegel

Benjamin "Bugsy" Siegel was born on Feb. 28, 1906. Growing up with little money in Brooklyn, New York, he and his friends Meyer Lansky and Morris "Moe Sedway lived a life that mimicked organized crime. Bugsy managed to establish himself as a teenage thug. They terrorized local street vendors and collected protection money from other gangs in the area.

Not too long after, they had a business that included bootlegging and gambling all over New York City and quickly rose through the ranks of the crime world. In 1937, Bugsy and Sedway were sent to California to build up the Mob's presence on the West Coast. Since bootlegging was no longer needed, Bugsy focused on gambling. He invested in the SS Rex, a gambling ship that was docked three miles off the coast of Santa Monica, Calif., to try and avoid California's anti-gambling laws.

When authorities closed the ship down, Bugsy turned his sights to Las Vegas since Nevada had legalized gambling, and they would avoid any headaches trying to dodge police.. with syndicate money in 1945, Bugsy took over a struggling construction project outside the city limits, the Flamingo Hotel and Casino. At that time, Las Vegas was nothing like the glittering city we think of today. The Flamingo was the first luxury hotel on the strip. Even though the project wasn't finished, Bugsy opened the casino on December 26, 1946. Celebrities like Judy Garland and Clark Gable attended the opening.

After the party was over, Bugsy closed the doors to finish construction, and the Mob back on the East Coast became antsy. By this time, the casino's budget had ballooned from $1 million to $6 million thanks to Bugsy skimming from the top. During a meeting of mob bigwigs in Cuba, it was settled that if the Flamingo were a success, Bugsy would be able to make things right. Luckily for Bugsy, the Flamingo had already made $250,000 in profit. Unluckily for Bugsy, it wasn't enough to please the Mob.

On June 20, 1947, Bugsy was sitting on the couch at his mistress Virginia Hill's home in Beverly Hills, California. At around 10:45 p.m., from a rose-covered pergola just 14 feet away from Bugsy, a .30-caliber military rifle fired at least nine shots at the mobster. Four rounds hit Bugsy, killing him instantly. Moments later, three of Meyer Lansky's henchmen walked into the Flamingo and declared they were taking over the casino. Beverly Hills Police Chief Clinton H. Anderson said in a statement at the time: "We spent many man-hours investigating the Siegel case and were convinced that he was killed by his own associates. But there was never sufficient evidence to pinpoint the assassin's identity."

Related: Where Convicted Criminal and 'Most Hated Man on the Internet' Hunter Moore Is Today

27. The Jamison Family Disappearance

On October 8, 2009, the Jamison family, 44-year-old Bobby Dale, 40-year-old Sherilyn Leighann, and their six-year-old daughter, Madyson Stormy Star, were seen for the last time before vanishing without a trace. The family lived in Eufaula, Okla., and was last seen by a man who lived in the mountains in southeastern Oklahoma. However, the witness claimed that he only saw the family and no one else in that area during the time.

The Jamisons were there to view a 40-acre plot of land that they were looking to purchase. They were looking to live in a shipping container they had already been living in on their plot of land in Eufaula. On October 16, eight days after the Jamisons were last seen alive, the first major discovery in the case occurred. Hunters in a remote location in the woods about a quarter-mile away from the last spot the Jamisons were seen discovered the Jamisons abandoned truck, which was still locked. Inside the truck, investigators found Bobby's wallet, Sherilyn's purse, jackets, a GPS, Bobby's cell phone, $32,000 cash in a bank bag, and

Jamison's pet dog, Maisy, who was incredibly malnourished but still alive.

Bobby's cellphone had a picture of Madyson, which is believed to have been taken the day before they disappeared. The truck showed no evidence of any kind of struggle. Former Sheriff Beauchamp remarked, "I think they were forced to stop and got out of the truck to meet with someone they recognized. And I think they either left willingly or by force." The GPS unit in the truck indicated that the family had been farther up a nearby hill prior to the location where the truck and belongings were found. Investigators followed the coordinates and found footprints.

One day later, on October 17, 300 people, including authorities and volunteers, staged a large-scale air and ground search party, but unfortunately, any leads went cold. The search for the Jamisons was called off. On November 16, 2013, hunters were scouting for deer hunting locations when they found partial skeletal remains of three bodies: two adults and one child. The remains were found less than three miles from where the Jamison family had parked their truck four years earlier. The search uncovered shoes, bits of clothing, adult teeth, an adult arm, and leg bone and bone fragments. The bones would eventually be confirmed as the missing Jamison family. However, no cause of death was determined, and the circumstances surrounding their disappearance remain unknown.

Related: Chris Watts' Horrifying Confession Letters

28. The O.J. Simpson Case

On June 13, 1994, the bodies of Nicole Brown Simpson – the ex-wife of football superstar O.J. Simpson and Ronald L. Goldman were found outside Nicole's townhouse, stabbed to death. At the time, Nicole and O.J. were divorced and living in separate residences. The bodies were found by neighbors who were literally led to the bodies by Nicole's dog, who was reported to be incessantly barking around the time of the murders.

The timeline surrounding the murders is as follows:

- On June 12, at 6:30 p.m., Nicole, her children, and others arrive at the restaurant called Mezzaluna.

- At 9:15 p.m. the same night, her sister called the restaurant to say that her mother had left her glasses there. Ronald Goldman goes to pick up the glasses.

- At 9–9:30 p.m., O.J. Simpson and his friend Brian "Kato" Kaelin head to a nearby McDonald's for dinner.

- At 9:45 p.m., they return home from McDonald's. Kato was staying at O.J. 's guest house at that time.

- At 9:48–9:50 p.m., Goldman leaves Mezzaluna with a white envelope containing the glasses.

- At 10:15 p.m., Nicole's neighbor heard a dog bark and cry while he was watching TV. Prosecutors then theorize that these barks signalized the murder of the dog's owner, Nicole.

- At 10:25 p.m., a limo driver named Allan Park arrives at O.J. Simpson's home. O.J. was scheduled for a red-eye flight at 11:45 p.m.

- At 10:40 p.m., Kato reported he heard three loud thumps on an outside wall of the guest house he was staying in.

- From 10:40–10:55 p.m., Allan Park buzzed O.J.'s intercom several times, but there was no answer.

- Just before 11 p.m., Allan reported seeing a shadowy figure that was 6'0" tall and over 200 pounds walking across the driveway.

- At 11 p.m., Allan tried buzzing OJ again; this time, O.J. answered. He claimed that he had overslept and just got out of the shower.

- At 11:45 p.m., OJ departs on his flight, and at 12:10 a.m. the next morning, the bodies of Nicole and Ronald Goldman are discovered.

Evidence found at the crime scene included a blood-stained glove, a knitted hat, and a bloodied footprint. When O.J. landed in Chicago, he was contacted by Detective Ron Phillips and told that his ex-wife had died. Upon hearing the news, O.J. asked, "Who killed her?" O.J. was then questioned for three hours by the LAPD.

On June 17, O.J. was charged with two counts of murder and declared a fugitive. The high-speed chase involving police and O.J. 's white Ford Bronco has been a lasting memory for anyone involved with the case. During the chase, O.J. sat in the passenger seat while his friend Al Cowlings drove. Cowlings reported that he didn't stop because "O.J. was holding a gun to [his] head" and that O.J. was "suicidal." The chase ended at O.J. 's home in Brentwood, Calif.

They found makeup adhesive, a fake mustache, O.J. 's passport, and a gun inside the car. What followed was one of the most publicized trials in US history. O.J. was represented by a high-profile defense team, also known as the "Dream Team," initially led by Robert Shapiro and Johnnie Cochran. The team also included F. Lee Bailey, Alan Dershowitz, Robert Kardashian, Shawn Holley, Carl E. Douglas, and Gerald Uelmen. Barry Scheck and Peter

Neufeld were two additional attorneys who specialized in DNA evidence. Prosecutors were Deputy District Attorneys Marcia Clark, William Hodgman, and later Christopher Darden.

They thought they had a strong case against Simpson, but Cochran convinced the jury that there was reasonable doubt concerning the validity of the state's DNA evidence, which was a new form of evidence in trials at that time. The reasonable doubt theory included evidence that lab scientists and technicians had allegedly mishandled the blood sample. The defense team also cited other misconduct by the LAPD related to systemic racism and incompetence. The verdict was released on October 3, 1995, and O.J. Simpson was acquitted. To this day, no other suspects have been questioned, and the murders remain unsolved.

Related: How Cuba Gooding, Jr. Approached the Role of O.J. Simpson

29. The Mystery of Overtoun Bridge

The Overtoun Bridge in Dumbarton, Scotland, seems to call dogs to jump to their death. Since the early 1960s, over 50 canines have perished, and hundreds more have leaped but survived, with some returning for a second leap onto the jagged rocks that lie 58 feet below. The Scottish Society for the Prevention of Cruelty to Animals has sent representatives to investigate the bridge but had no luck.

In terms of scientific truth, it is debatable whether dogs are capable of forming a suicide attempt. Yet, something is luring dogs off the Overtoun Bridge, often from the same spot and always on sunny, dry days. Many theories have emerged, including that the bridge is haunted, a small animal is marking the area with an irresistible scent, or a sound exists below the bridge that only dogs can hear. Whatever is causing this phenomenon, dog owners crossing this bridge would be wise to take extra caution and keep their dogs on leashes.

30. Malaysia Airlines Flight 370 Disappearance

On March 8, 2014, while flying from Malaysia to China, a Boeing 777 carrying 239 passengers and crew members vanished into thin air. The largest global search effort in aviation history only turned up a mere 20 pieces of aircraft debris. However, the Prime Minister of Malaysia declined to comment other than to say that the aircraft disappeared over the Indian Ocean.

The lack of closure has propelled multiple theories, including a hijacking, a United States capture, a crew suicide (it was reported later that the pilot was having marital problems), a fire aboard the aircraft, vertical entry into the ocean, a meteor strike and even an alien abduction.

Despite the passage of time and the e $160 million spent scouring thousands of square miles of ocean, the disappearance of Malaysian Airlines Flight 370 and the fate of the 239 people aboard remains a mystery.

Related: Inside Convicted Killer Scott Peterson's Life Behind Bars

31. The Peculiar Death of Charles C. Morgan

On March 22, 1977, escrow agent Charles Morgan went missing after leaving his home in Phoenix, Arizona. Three days later, he finally returned home around 2 a.m. His wife, Ruth, reported that he had a plastic handcuff around one ankle and handcuffs around his hands. He pointed to his throat, indicating that he couldn't speak, so his wife handed him a pen and paper, and he wrote that there was a hallucinogenic drug in his throat that could destroy his nervous system.

Ruth wanted to get in contact with the police or a physician, but Charles told her not to and said it would put their family in danger. As Ruth nursed him back to health, he disclosed that he had been working as a secret agent for the US Treasury Department for the past two to three years. He then claimed his abductors took his treasury ID and provided no more details.

Two months after his initial disappearance, he was reported to be missing again. After nine days, Ruth received a phone call from an unidentified woman who said, "Chuck is alright. Ecclesiastes 12, 1 through 8," and then hung up. Two days after the strange phone call, on June 18, his body was discovered lying 40 miles west of Tucson near his car. Charles had been shot in the back of the head by his own gun. He was found wearing a bulletproof vest, a belt buckle that had a hidden knife, and a holster. A pair of sunglasses that didn't belong to him was found at the scene.

Investigators searched his car and found several weapons and a cache of ammunition. The car had also been altered so that it could be unlocked from the fender. On the rear seat of the car, Morgan's tooth, wrapped up in a white handkerchief, was discovered. There was also a $2 bill with several Spanish surnames and a map of the border area pinned to Morgan's underwear. The map led to Robles Junction and Felicity, the area between Tucson and Mexico. Those towns had a reputation for smuggling at the time.

Above the surnames, "Ecclesiastes 12" was written, and an arrow was drawn to the bill's serial number pointing to the numbers 1 and 8. Some of the other writings on the bill had alleged Masonic references. Charles also had a piece of paper with directions in his handwriting that led to the site where he was found. Medical examiners claimed that Charles Morgan was only dead for 12 hours when he was found. Strangely, there were no fingerprints found on the scene, not even on the gun. On Morgan's hands, they found gunpowder and residue.

For this reason, the sheriff's department labeled the death a suicide that seemed to be the end of the Charles C. Morgan case. Ruth Morgan staunchly rejected this theory and held the belief that he was murdered. "I don't know if this will ever be solved," she said. "I'd like to know why. I don't think we'll ever find out who killed him."

Related: The Best Murder Mystery Movies

32. The Disappearance of Walter Collins

On March 10, 1928, nine-year-old Walter Collins donned a lumber jacket, brown corduroy trousers, black Oxfords, and a grey cap and set off to see a movie in the Mount Washington neighborhood of Los Angeles. Walter never returned home. His mother, Christine Collins, a telephone operator, reported her son missing 5 days later on March 15.

At the time, the area was still recovering from the kidnapping and gruesome murder of a 12-year-old girl, Marion Parker, that had only happened three months earlier. Tips of apparent Walter sightings came from as far away as San Francisco and even Oakland, Calif. In one bizarre tip, someone reported seeing Walter at a gas station in Glendale with his body wrapped in newspaper and only his head visible. Police searched for months without any success.

In Illinois in August 1928, state police picked up a runaway boy who matched Walter's description. The boy told authorities he was Walter Collins and gave a hazy description of his abduction. He spoke to Christine over the phone, and she paid $76 to have her son transported back to Los Angeles. The boy lived with Christine for three weeks when she realized that this boy wasn't her son. Christine found that the boy who was living with her was an inch shorter than Walter, and she used dental records to show that this was a different kid. Christine told the police, "Yes, he looks like Walter. And, in some ways, acts like my son. But still, I'm not certain about it. You see, Walter was quiet and well-behaved. He always called me 'Mother.' This child calls me 'Ma,' and at times, he is hard to handle. I certainly hope that he is my son somehow; I just can't bring myself to believe it."

Pressured by the public, the police insisted that the child was indeed Walter. They conducted a series of tests to prove it. They had the child find his way back home from memory and bring in Walter's pet dog, who allegedly recognized the boy as its owner. Nevertheless, Christine wasn't convinced. LAPD captain J.J. Jones accosted the grieving mother, saying, "What are you trying to do, make fools out of us all? Or are you trying to shirk your duties as a mother and have the state provide for your son? You are the most cruel-hearted woman I have ever known. You are a fool!"

On September 8, 1928, the police had Christine committed to the psychiatric ward at the Los Angeles County General Hospital. While Christine was in the hospital, JJ spoke again to the boy that they had picked up in Illinois. During that conversation, the boy made it known that he was, indeed, not Walter Collins, but instead Arthur Hutchins. After his mother had died, the boy ran away from his father and stepmother. He was hitchhiking around the US, and when he was inside a cafe, he was told that he resembled a missing boy from Los Angeles. When he was picked up, juvenile authorities were skeptical about his story, but the police were so desperate to close the Collins case that they insisted on its accuracy. As for why Arthur lied, he said that he wanted to go to Hollywood to meet a cowboy actor named Tom Mix.

Christine was released from the psych ward on September 13, 1928, and sued the LAPD. J.J. Jones was suspended from duty. Collins won her lawsuit against Jones and was awarded $10,800, which he never paid. She spent the rest of her life continuing to search for her missing son. This mystery inspired the movie The Changeling, which starred Angelina Jolie.

Related: What Sarma Melngailis Is Doing Post-Bad Vegan

33. The Unexplained Phoenix Lights

On March 13, 1997, a string of five lights in a V formation appeared in the sky above Phoenix, Ariz. The National UFO Reporting Center reported that the first call about the lights came in at around 8:16 p.m. from a retired police officer in Paulden, Arizona, which is about two hours north of Phoenix. After that, the National UFO Reporting Center began to receive a slew of calls south of Paulden, suggesting that the lights were moving in a southeastern direction. There were more than 700 alleged witnesses who saw the lights, including pilots, police officers, and military officials who lit up the National UFO Reporting Center's switchboard, demanding explanations. Some described the lights as orbs, others said triangles.

However, a large number of witnesses described the lights as part of a singular, massive craft that made no noise. Around 10 p.m., a second set of as many as nine lights appeared in the sky. A laser printer technician named Dana Valentine claimed to have witnessed the craft from his yard in Phoenix. "We could see the outline of the mass behind the lights, but you couldn't actually see the mass," he reported. "It was more like a gray distortion of the night sky, wavy. I don't know exactly what it was, but I know it's not a technology the public has heard before."

Air traffic controllers could not see the lights on the radar despite seeing them in the sky with their own eyes. Frances Barwood, the 1997 Phoenix city councilwoman who launched an investigation into the event, said that of the over 708 witnesses she interviewed, "The government never interviewed even one." To this day, the unexplained Phoenix lights remain a mystery.

Related: Fact or Fiction? 16 of the Most Chilling UFO Sightings Ever Reported Throughout History

34. The Eerie Lady of the Dunes

On July 26, 1974, 12-year-old Leslie Metcalfe was returning from the beach with her family in Provincetown, Massachusetts. A local dog had followed them, and when it took off barking, Leslie broke away from her parents and started to go after it. In the dunes of Racepoint Beach, a mile east of a ranger station, Leslie found the decomposing body of a naked woman.

The woman was 5 "6" weighed about 145 pounds, and was between 20 and 40 years old. She was lying on one side of a beach towel, with her head resting on a pair of jeans and a blue bandana. It was estimated that the body had been lying there for anywhere from 10 days to three weeks before being discovered. The left side of her head was crushed, and she had almost been completely decapitated. While no weapons were found, it was believed that a military entrenching tool was used almost to cut off her head. Her hands were removed, ostensibly to conceal the woman's identity through fingerprints.

Due to the horrific state of the body, authorities believed that the woman was murdered. With no sign of struggle at the time, authorities believed that the unidentified victim would have known her murderer. The only signs of evidence were the size-10 footprints that indicated a heavy person running away. Provincetown Police Chief Jimmy Meads said, "The killer likely drove the victim to the dune in a 4-wheel-drive sand vehicle to sunbathe."

Despite using bloodhounds and missing person bulletins, scouring the registers of local lodgings, and looking into anyone who had a permit to bring their vehicle onto the beach, police turned up nothing. In 2019, Provincetown local Margie Childs reflected on the case, saying, "The fact that no one could identify the lady of the dunes in the tight-knit community was very strange."

Almost 50 years later, the victim, known as the Lady of the Dunes, is still unidentified.

Related: Where Is Jodi Arias Now?

35. The Case of Mary Reeser

On July 2, 1951, in Saint Petersburg, Fla., Mary Hardy Reeser was visited by her son, Dr. Richard Reeser, in her apartment. Mary had told her son that she had taken two mild sedatives that were mainly used to calm patients before surgery. She had also told him she was planning to take two more before bed. Later that night, she would fall asleep in an upholstered chair for the last time as she would become the victim of an apparent house fire.

The next morning, Mary's landlord reported smelling smoke around 5 a.m., but it wasn't until 8 a.m. when she went to deliver a telegraph to Mary that she would smell the smoke again. She discovered soot in the hallway, and the doorknob leading to Mary's apartment was too hot to grab, so she enlisted the help of nearby house painters to get into the apartment. What they found inside the apartment was truly horrifying: The remains of Mary Reeser. Her skull was reportedly shrunk to the size of a cup, and parts of her spine also remained. However, the most terrifying was that Mary's left foot was still in its black satin slipper, the skin unburned. The rest of her remains had been completely cremated.

What makes the case odd was the environment of her surroundings. For a body to be cremated, the body must burn at 3,000 degrees Fahrenheit for three to four hours. Somehow, the surrounding area of her chair and the rest of her apartment were unaffected. The walls had no burn marks and showed no signs of scorching or burned paint. Light switches were melted, but the outlets were still completely functional. Candlesticks had melted, but their wicks stood upright, and a stack of newspapers close to the chair was undamaged.

Mary's neighbors were also unaware of the fire. The FBI eventually declared that Mary had been incinerated by the wick effect when the clothing of the victim soaks up melted human fat and acts like the wick of a candle. As she was a known user of sleeping pills, they hypothesized that she had fallen unconscious while smoking and set fire to her nightclothes. However, there is still some speculation that she died of spontaneous human combustion. Related: The Best True Crime Shows on Streaming

36. Escape from Alcatraz

Alcatraz Federal Penitentiary Robert Alexander/Getty Images Formerly a military base, the high-security prison Alcatraz sat on a 22-acre island known as "The Rock" about 1.25 miles from San Francisco. Because of this, the prison was deemed "inescapable." The water surrounding the prison hovers around 48 to 54 degrees yearly and has strong currents. The prison would fall into disrepair as time passed, and the budget to fix numerous problems was limited. This would become a resounding factor in the inmates, Clarence Anglin, John Anglin, Allen West, and Frank Morris, escaping.

It was reported that West approached Morris with the plan to escape in early 1960. West knew of a ventilator cover in Cell Block B that might not have been sealed with concrete like most vents. If this was true, it could give them a way to get on the prison roof from the inside. West also began working with the maintenance crew, which provided him insight into the building's structure, layout, and weaknesses.

By September 1961, the Anglin brothers, John and Clarence, Morris, and West requested cell moves that made them closer to each other in Cell Block B, directly under the unsecured vent. All cell moves were approved. The plan to escape was undoubtedly bold and ingenious. Phase 1 involved creating a head start to provide them enough time to tackle the mile and a quarter to San Francisco. They created a diversion by painting dummy heads made from a plaster-like mix of soap, concrete, and other materials, complete with real human hair. They laid their heads in their beds to fool the guards. Sure enough, when the 7 a.m. bell went off to wake the prisoners on the morning after the escape, guards discovered that the prisoners were still "asleep" in their beds.

It wasn't until one of the guards reached into Morris's cell, pushed the head, and it fell onto the ground that the guards realized that something was wrong. To this day, the dummy head still bears the damage that resulted from the fall. It's unknown who came up with the idea to make dummy heads; Clarence worked as a barber and had access to hair trimmings. After laying the dummy heads in their beds, the gang moved on to phase two of their plans to escape the inescapable prison. The men went to work on busting out of their cells. All four had 5x9 inch ventilation grates in the back of their cells. Perhaps from his time in maintenance, West knew that the wall surrounding the grates was less than six inches thick, making it possible for each man to expand the hole in their cell to fit through.

For months, the prisoners spent time drilling small, close-knit holes around the cover of the ventilation grates using crude handmade tools like spoons stolen from the kitchen and a drill made from a vacuum cleaner motor. These holes made it possible to remove the entire small section of the wall around the air vents, which they covered with their musical instruments or fake covers made of cardboard. These holes allowed them to access a utility corridor directly behind their cells and typically left unguarded. From there, they could climb up to a hidden land area directly above their cellblock, where they had been working secretly for several months. In this area, they could make the dummy heads, tools, and other items they'd use in their great escape. However, it's worth noting that West never reached this landing spot during the escape because he could not break through the last portion of the wall around his ventilation grate.

Consequently, he was left behind. From the landing, the trio could climb pipes to the ceiling and reach an air vent they had previously pried off to ready their escape.

Experts say that a sound that was heard around 10:30 p.m. was the sound of the air vent cover being pushed off on the roof. They then climbed down the roof via a pipe to the back of their cell block, climbed the 15-foot fence, and made their way to the island's north shore. To escape the island, the prisoners had made life preservers and a 14-foot rubber raft, all made from prison-issued raincoats. They gathered over 50 raincoats for the job, possibly stitched them together using sewing machines, and vulcanized the rubber coats by holding the seams up to the heat from the steam pipes.

The raft was inflated by using a concertina. Once it was realized that the prisoners were missing, Alcatraz went into lockdown as a search began. Guards quickly found the hidden workshop, the hole in the ceiling, and footprints on the roof and ground of the pipe where they climbed down. The FBI joined the case, as well as the Coast Guard and the Bureau of Prison Authorities, in a wide-scale search, but the escapees, as well as their raft, were never seen again.

Related: Who Is Roy Radin and How Is He Connected to the Son of Sam?

37. The Sheppard Murder Case

On Feb. 21, 1945, Dr. Samuel Sheppard and Marilyn Reese were married and settled in a small, close-knit, friendly community near Lake Erie, Ohio. They had their first and only child two years later, whom they affectionately nicknamed Chip. Samuel was a respected neurosurgeon, and the couple was believed to have a happy marriage. On July 3, 1954, the Sheppards hosted a party for their neighbors that included dinner, drinks, and a movie. Just after midnight, Samuel fell asleep on the couch, and Marilyn said her goodbyes to the guests.

At about 5:30 a.m. on July 4, Mayor Spencer Houk, a close friend of the Sheppards, woke to a phone call from Samuel saying, "My God, Spence, get over here quick. I think they've killed Marilyn." Houk and his wife Esther made a beeline towards the house to find Samuel shirtless in his study, holding his neck in a seeming state of shock. They called the police, and the authorities arrived around 6 a.m. According to the police report, Marilyn's body was found lying upward with her face turned towards the door. She was beaten beyond recognition. She had over 20 gashes deep into her face and scalp. Sheets were covered with blood, and the walls were dripping with heavy spatter. Her pajamas were partially removed, leaving her exposed. The autopsy reported that her time of death was around 4:30 a.m.

Sadly, it also revealed that Marilyn had been four months pregnant with their second child. According to Samuel, he had been asleep downstairs when he heard Marilyn shout his name. He ran upstairs and found her being attacked by a "white form." They fought, but Samuel was hit on the back of his neck and knocked out. When he woke, Marilyn was dead, and the white form was gone. He then ran to Chip's room and saw him alive and sleeping soundly. He went downstairs and saw the white form exiting through the back door. He chased the tall and bushy-haired figure down to the shores of Lake Erie.

Samuel then explained that he "lunged or jumped and grasped" at the strange figure, but then he said, "I felt myself twisting or choking, and that terminated my consciousness." When Samuel came to, it was nearly dawn, and his shirt and watch were missing. Samuel was the only witness to the crime and the most likely suspect. On Dec. 21, 1954, after extensive deliberating for four days, the jury found Sheppard guilty of second-degree murder. He was sentenced to life in prison but staunchly maintained his innocence. Eventually, his life sentence was overturned;

the real story about what happened to Marilyn Sheppard remains a mystery.

38. The Killing of Ken Rex McElroy

In the sleepy small town of Skidmore, Mo., on July 10, 1981, Ken Rex McElroy was shot dead in the streets in broad daylight. There were 60 witnesses, but the crime remains unsolved to this day. McElroy grew up in a poor family and left school by the eighth grade. It was believed that he was possibly largely illiterate, and at 18 years old, he was injured by a metal slab falling on him at a construction site. The incident left him with chronic pain, and some attributed his sometimes bizarre and violent behavior to a head injury as a result of the accident. McElroy was reported as being a 270-pound giant of a man. A local farmer described him: "I think that Ken simply wanted to be big and important and have people afraid of him when he walked down the street. And he got that. They were."

McElroy made a decent living by leasing the land off his farm, trading and racing dogs, and allegedly stealing livestock, grain, alcohol, gasoline, and antiques. He was in constant trouble with the law. His lawyer estimated that he was charged with various crimes at least three times a year. By some counts, he was indicted as many as 21 times but escaped conviction all but once. McElroy used to brag that his lawyer, Richard Gene McFadin, also represented the Mob and would keep him out of jail.

Another tactic McElroy would use to avoid jail time was to intimidate witnesses by following them or parking outside their homes and watching them until they were no longer willing to testify. Some of his bigger crimes included robbery, harassing and assaulting women, destroying property, threatening lives, and shooting at least two people, all of which he avoided jail for. Police were also afraid of confronting McElroy since he was almost always heavily armed and didn't think twice before shooting a cop.

The people of Skidmore felt abandoned by the justice system that couldn't stop McElroy from causing havoc in their town. On April 25, 1988, in Ernest "Bo" Bowenkamp's general store, the store clerk, Evelyn Sumy, asked McElroy's eight-year-old daughter, Tanya, to return a piece of candy she didn't pay for. When McElroy learned of the situation, he became so enraged that he began stalking the Bowenkamp family. On July 8, 1980, McElroy drove to the alley behind the general store. Once there, he threatened Bo Bowenkamp and shot the 70-year-old grocer in the neck at close range with a shotgun. This was the second time he had shot someone; the first time was local farmer Romaine Henry, whom McElroy shot in the stomach after Henry chased him off of Henry's land.

Miraculously, Bo Bownkamp survived the shot, and McElroy was arrested and charged with attempted murder. His preliminary trial was set for Aug. 18, 1980, and, in his usual fashion, McElroy tried to intimidate the Bowenkamp family and supporters from testifying. Bowenkamp's wife said, "You can't know how intimidating it was after that. Before his trial, he'd drive to our house in his pickup at night and sit there. Sometimes, he would fire his gun. It was frightening."

Nevertheless, McElroy was able to delay the trial almost five months to June 25, 1981. During this time, the acting prosecuting attorney resigned, and a new prosecutor, David Baird, was assigned to the case. It is rumored that McElroy bullied the previous prosecutor into leaving. Baird was only three years out of law school but accomplished the impossible. He was able to convict McElroy of a crime, granted he was only convicted of second-degree assault.

The jury set a maximum sentence of two years, and the judge freed him on a $40,000 bail bond pending the appeal. This is because Baird lessened the charge from "attempt to kill" to "knowingly caused serious physical injury." Soon after he was released, he was bizarrely spotted with a rifle and bayonet at the town's local bar, D&G Tavern, where he was making graphic threats about killing Bo Bowenkamp. He was then arrested and then quickly released for violating bail by being armed. On July 10, 1981, there was a local meeting at the town's Legion Hall, just down the street from the D&G Tavern. As many as 60 residents attended, including the mayor and the sheriff. During the meeting, the whole topic of discussion was what they could do legally to prevent McElroy from harming anyone else.

County Sheriff Dan Estes suggested a neighborhood watch, but an attendee said the mindset perfectly: "We simply felt that the system had failed us. We all knew what McElroy was like, and there he was again and again. It seemed like no one could stop him." During the meeting, a local said they had spotted McElroy and his young wife, Trena, on their way to grab drinks at the D&G Tavern. The meeting was quickly adjourned, and the 60-odd people at that meeting quietly descended on the tavern, flanking McElroy's truck. Some attendees entered the bar and waited for McElroy to finish his drinks.

Upon returning to the truck, where Trena was sitting in the passenger seat, McElroy lit a cigarette. Trena then reported glancing over her shoulder and saw someone point a rifle towards the back of the truck and take aim at McElroy, and then shots were fired. McElroy was hit twice, killing him. In all, there were 46 potential witnesses to the shooting, including Trena. No one called for an ambulance. Only Trena claimed to identify a gunman. However, every other witness was unable to name the person who had pulled the trigger or claimed not to have seen who fired the fatal shots. The DA declined to press charges. To this day, the person who shot Ken McElroy remains unknown.

Related: How to Watch the Secrets of the Greco Family-and the Chilling True Story Behind the Series

39. The Michelle Von Emster Case

On April 15, 1994, in San Diego, Calif., around Sunset Cliffs, two surfers found the body of 25-year-old Michelle Von Emster floating face down in a kelp bed. The body was taken to the lifeguard headquarters. She was found naked, wearing only a brass bracelet and two rings. She had a butterfly tattoo on her shoulder and had long brown hair. Medical examiner Robert Engel also noted she had "large, tearing type wounds with missing tissue" as the body was missing most of its right leg. He believed that Michelle had not been in the water long and marked her cause of death as "unknown."

Nevertheless, there was an overwhelming consensus that her death was caused by a shark attack. One day later, on April 16, medical examiner Brian Blackbourne conducted a formal autopsy. In addition to her right leg being missing from the thigh down, Michelle's neck was broken "as if she had been in a car wreck," and she had broken ribs, scrapes, bruises, and contusions on her face. Blackbourne also reported finding sand in her mouth, throat, lungs, and stomach and that she was alive when the injuries were inflicted.

According to Blackbourne's timeline, he concluded that she got into the water around midnight and that this was a shark attack because lifeguards, harbor police, and marine biologists at Scripps Institution of Oceanography told him so. However, some things don't add up for the cause of death being a shark attack. Blackbourne had never seen a death caused by a shark before, and neither had anyone who initially saw the body. The experts at the Scripps Institution never saw Michelle's body, making their initial inquiries questionable.

Additionally, many experts, including Ralph Collier, the leading expert in Pacific Coast white shark behavior and ecology, say today that this death wasn't caused by a Great White as the autopsy stated. After seeing Michelle's body, Collier said, "When a shark bites off part of a limb, the break is clean, almost like you put it on a table saw. What remained of Michelle's femur was anything but. It looked like what happens when you get a piece of bamboo and whittle it down to a point with a knife. I've looked at close to 100 photos of cases I have reviewed over the years, and I've never seen any bones that came to a point."

Plus, it's important to note once Michelle's leg had been severed, she would have bled out quickly from a severed femoral artery. This would have made it extremely difficult to take a large breath, as she would have had to have done to get the sand into her stomach. This makes the theory that a shark forced her to the bottom of the ocean (where she took a breath and swallowed sand) extremely unlikely. Officially, Michelle's death is considered the result of a great white shark attack, but the true nature and circumstances of her untimely demise remain a mystery.

40. The Pollock Sisters

In the 1940s, Florence and John Pollock were married, and in 1946, after having two sons, they welcomed their first daughter, Joanna. In 1951, Florence gave birth to another baby girl named Jacqueline. Despite their age differences, the two girls had an extremely close bond. Joanna liked to take care of Jacqueline and saw herself as the ultimate big sister. Since their mother was busy running the family's grocery delivery business, Joanna saw herself as a second mother to her little sister. They enjoyed playing dress-up and pretend and generally enjoyed being around each other.

Eerily, Joanna would always state that she would never grow up to become a lady. She would always say that she would remain a child forever. No one took her seriously and chalked it to the child's creative imagination. On May 7, 1957, six-year-old Jacqueline and 11-year-old Joanna walked to church with a young neighborhood boy as they often did. While they were walking, a car came up behind them and hit them, going at an incredibly high speed, killing all three of the children.

The Pollock sisters died instantly, and the little boy they were with died from his injuries at the hospital. The woman who was driving the car had just lost her children in a custody battle and was feeling angry and upset and was trying to take her own life. When learning about her children's deaths, Florence fell into a deep depression that lasted quite a long time. On the other hand, John believed that the girls were in ven or that they'd be reincarnated. He said he would have dreams about the girls and felt some presence in their bedroom. He claimed that whenever he went in there, he felt like he wasn't alone.

John was always fascinated with reincarnation and prayed to God to bring his daughters back. On the other hand, Florence was a very strict Catholic and never toyed with any of John's notions about reincarnation. This strained their relationship so much that they almost got divorced. However, they stayed together and got pregnant again. From the beginning of the pregnancy, John thought there were two babies despite the doctor only claiming one. However, John would keep insisting that there were two, and the doctor was proved wrong on the day that twins Gillian and Jennifer were born on Oct. 4, 1958.

Twins never ran in the family, and Florence never felt like she had two fetuses growing inside her. Eerily, the newborn twins had the exact same birthmarks that Joanna and Jacqueline had, and it was this that Florence started to consider her husband's beliefs seriously.

When the twins were old enough to talk, they began identifying and requesting toys belonging to their sisters who had passed on and would point out landmarks that only Joanna and Jaqueline knew, like the school they attended. They would sometimes panic upon seeing cars and knew about street safety without their parents telling them about it.

The story of the Pollock Sisters went to Dr. Ian Stevenson, a psychologist who studied reincarnation. After studying thousands of reincarnation cases, Dr. Stevenson wrote a book about 14 cases he believed to have been real, including that of the Pollock Sisters. Whether or not the actual occurrence of reincarnation exists has yet to be explained.

41. The Disappearance of Paula Jean Welden

On Dec. 1, 1946, a sophomore at Bennington College, 18-year-old Paula Jean Welden, told her roommate, Elizabeth Parker, she was going for a long walk but failed to return to the shared space. Local witnesses reported seeing her on the 270-mile trail called Vermont's Long Trail that cuts through Vermont to the Canadian border. A search party was immediately formed, but no clues were found on the trail. Soon after, The Bennington Banner reported that "tantalizing and unquestionably strange leads" began to materialize. There was one in particular made by a Massachusetts waitress that she'd served an agitated young woman matching Paula's description. Upon learning of this lead, Paula's father disappeared for 36 hours, supposedly in pursuit of the lead.

Nevertheless, the authorities thought it was strange, and it led to him becoming a prime suspect in Paula's disappearance. Stories began circulating that Paula's home life was not nearly as idyllic and picturesque as her parents had initially reported to the police. Paula had not returned home for Thanksgiving the week prior, and she may have been upset about a disagreement with her father. While claiming his innocence, Paula's father posited a theory that

Paula was distraught about a boy she liked at school and that perhaps the boy should have been a suspect.

Over the next decade after Paula's disappearance, a local Bennington man twice ragged to friends that he knew where Paula's body was buried. However, he was unable to lead the police to anybody. With no evidence of a crime, nobody, and no forensic clues, the case grew cold, and the fate of Paula Jean Welden was never discovered.

Related: Where Is Chris Watts Now? How the Convicted Wife and Child Killer Spends His Time Behind Bars

42. The Disappearance of the Flannan Isles Lighthouse Keepers

The Flannan Isles is a group of rocky, uninhabited islands off the Western coast of Scotland. The islands are best known for being adored by sheep, and shepherds often sail their flock there to graze. Sheep grazed on the Flannan Isles were believed to give birth to twins or recover from illness. Despite it being a paradise for the woolly critters, rumors of a haunted spirit prevented shepherds from ever staying overnight.

In 1896, the Board of Trade funded the construction of a lighthouse on the largest of the Flannan Isles, Eilean Mor. In December 1899, the lighthouse was completed and lit for the first time. Four lighthouse keepers were assigned to maintain the lighthouse and work a rotation of six weeks on and two weeks off. This meant there were always three men on the island simultaneously. In mid-December 1900, the three men on the island were 43-year-old principal keeper James Ducat, who had a wife, four children, and 20 years experience; the 40-year-old occasional keeper, Donald MacArthur, who was married and covering for the first assistant keeper who was on sick leave and the 28-year-old second assistant keeper, Thomas Marshall.

The fourth keeper, Joseph Moore, was off duty. Around midnight on Dec. 15, the steamship Archtor passed by the Isles. Captain Holman noticed he could not see the light from the lighthouse even though the conditions should have allowed him to. When the Archtor arrived in port, they reported the light's absence even though this was never communicated to the Northern Lighthouse Board. On Dec. 26, the lighthouse tender ship Hesperus regularly visited Eilean Mor.

When nearing the island, Captain James Harvey found it odd that the Scottish flag had been removed from the flagpole. He then sounded the horn to get the attention of the three lighthouse keepers, but there was no response. They then attempted firing a flare, but again, no response. Joseph Moore was on board the Hesperus, and with no signal coming from the island, he was sent ashore. Upon arriving at Eilean Mor's east landing, nothing appeared amiss, and everything seemed normal just as he had left it. He went up the island to find the entrance gate and the entrance door, and after that, the door was all shut. However, the kitchen door was found open, and it was discovered that the fire had not been lit for several days. All of the clocks were stopped.

"I then entered the rooms in succession," Moore reported. "I found the beds empty just as they had left them early." The bodies of the three men were never found, and their disappearance still remains a mystery to this day.

43. The Murder of Betty Shanks

On Sept. 19, 1952, 22-year-old Betty Shanks got off the train at Days Road Terminus in Grange, a suburb of Brisbane, Queensland, Australia. She attended classes at the University of Queensland and started her short walk home after getting off a train. However, she would never arrive. Her badly beaten body was found on the corner of Carberry and Thomas Streets in the garden of a house at 5:35 a.m. the next morning by a policeman who lived nearby. At the time, it became one of Queensland's most notorious investigations ever.

Despite many theories, her murder is still unsolved. As of today, there is still a $50,000 AUS reward for a suspect.

44. The Leatherman

The Leatherman was a particular vagabond famous for wearing his handmade leather clothes and traveled an annual route between the Connecticut River and the Hudson River, roughly from 1857 to 1889. His repeating voyage took him to certain towns in western Connecticut and eastern New York, and he would return to each town every 34 to 36 days. Living in rock shelters, he stopped at towns along his 365-mile loop for food and supplies. It was unclear what he did for work. One shopkeeper recorded his usual store order: "One loaf of bread, a can of sardines, one pound of fancy crackers, a pie, two quarts of coffee, one gill of brandy, and a bottle of beer."

An article from the Burlington Free Press dated April 7th, 1870, refers to him as the "Leather-Clad Man" and states that he rarely spoke and that when people addressed him, he would simply speak in monosyllables. According to rumors, he was from Picardy, France. Even though he was fluent in French, he communicated mostly with grunts and gestures, rarely using the little English he knew. When asked about his background, he would abruptly end the conversation. Even after his death from cancer in 1889, the Leatherman's true identity remains unknown and a mystery.

Related: How to Watch the Casey Anthony Docuseries Casey Anthony: Where the Truth Lies

45. The Severed Feet Mystery

In 2007, a girl was walking along a beach in British Columbia when she found a sneaker that had washed up onshore. To her horror, she found that a human foot was inside. Since then, some severed feet have washed ashore since then belonging to five men, one woman, and three of unknown sex. The case remains a mystery throughout the years, with many theories floating around the general public and the media as to who the feet belonged to.

The Vancouver police managed to identify one foot in 2008, matching its DNA to a man who was described as suicidal. The authorities were then able to match two other found feet to a woman who was also believed to have committed suicide. Because of these findings, many speculate that the feet belong to those who jumped off a bridge to their deaths. However, because of the rarity of only feet and no other body parts showing up, some believe they were those of the victims of the tsunami in 2004 since the makes of all of the shoes were manufactured before 2004. Whatever the source these feet are coming from, they have left the world (and authorities) stumped.

46. The Case of Jeanette DePalma

In 1972, in Springfield, New Jersey, a dog brought a decomposing forearm to its owner. They quickly alerted the police, and this prompted a police search. A body was soon found afterward atop a cliff. The body was identified as Jeanette DePalmer, a 16-year-old girl who was missing for six weeks.

The Satanic panic grew fast and fierce. The hill where she was discovered was covered with occult symbols, and many were led to believe that her body was placed on a makeshift altar. Many locals and even some police officers pointed their fingers at an alleged coven of witches who were rumored to have used DePalma for a human sacrifice; others said it was a Satanic group. Because of a flood, many of the case's details have been destroyed. However, some reports from local papers mention that police couldn't determine the cause of death due to the body's decomposition. Authorities investigated a local homeless man who was a prime suspect only to find no connection to the killing. Many believed that DePalma may have provoked a group of Satan-worshipping teens at her high school since she was involved with a group that helped drug addicts find their faith in Christ. To this day, her death remains unsolved.

Related: The Biggest Bombshells From Casey Anthony: Where the Truth Lies

47. The Vanishing of Cynthia Anderson

Cynthia Anderson, 20, was raised in a very religious household that followed a schedule filled with prayer meetings, swimming events, camping events, seasonal parties, and Sunday worship, all organized by the church. She and her family attended. Cynthia's father, Michael Andersen, described his daughter as a "quiet and obedient kind of girl who never made waves yet had lots of friends." Cynthia was also a very attractive young woman, and even though her parents had very strict rules, she had a boyfriend who was also a church member.

That summer, her father reported that Cynthia was "spending a lot of time on her face and becoming a bit of a debutante." Cynthia worked as a legal secretary in Toledo, Ohio, but was preparing to quit to attend Bible College, the same one her boyfriend attended. By the way, her job was going, and her last day couldn't come soon enough. The previous year, on a wall across from Cynthia's desk that was viewable from outside the window, someone had spray-painted the words "I Love You Cindy" in large letters with smaller "by GW" in the corner. Cynthia was the only "Cindy" on that side of the strip mall where the graffiti was located.

It seemed intentionally placed so that only Cynthia could see it. However, Cynthia had no idea who GW could have been. The message remained there for six months until it was eventually covered up. This time, The message appeared in bigger letters, but it became the least of Cynthia's problems. During the summer of 1981, Cynthia was being harassed by some anonymous phone calls with disturbing messages. This frightened her, and she began experiencing nightmares about being attacked by a man. It got so bad that her job even installed an emergency buzzer at her desk, and she kept her office doors locked at all times. Unfortunately, these precautions wouldn't be enough. On Aug. 4, 1981, Cynthia skipped breakfast and left her parent's house around 8:30 a.m. to go to work. She arrived at the law office and was seen as late as 9:45 a.m.

Around lunchtime, her employer, James Rabbitt, arrived at the office. The lights and radio were on, but no sign of Cynthia. The scent of nail polish remover hung in the air; there was no note, and the phones were still ringing off the hook. There were no signs of a struggle; according to reports, the office door was still locked from the inside. Her car was still in the parking lot, but her keys and purse were missing. Eerily, a romance novel that Cynthia was reading was left open at her desk to a page where the protagonist was abducted at knifepoint. Cynthia Andersen was never found, and her case remains unsolved.

48. The Disappearance of Kyron Horman

On June 4, 2010, his stepmother Terri dropped seven-year-old Kyron Horman off at Skyline Elementary School in Portland, Oregon. She stayed with him as he attended the school's science fair, walked him down the hall to his class, and left the school around 8:45 a.m. However, he was never seen in his first class and was instead marked absent that day. At 3:30 p.m., Terri and her husband, Kyron's father, Kaine, walked with their daughter to the bus stop to meet Kyron. However, the bus driver told them that the boy had not boarded the bus after school and to call the school to ask where he might be.

Terri rang the school, only to be informed by the school secretary that, as far as anyone there knew, Kyron had not been at school and had been marked absent. Realizing then that the boy was missing, the secretary called the police.

The search party for Kyron was extensive and primarily focused on the two-mile radius around Skyline Elementary and Sauvie Island, which lies six miles away. The search for Kyron, which happened over a span of 10 days, was the largest in Oregon history and included over

1,300 searchers from Oregon, Washington, and California. A reward posted for information leading to the discovery of Kyron, initially $25,000, rose to $50,000 in July 2010.

Despite the long search, no evidence was ever found. Legal proceedings, including a lawsuit from Kyron's mother, Desiree Young, alleging that Terri Horman is responsible for the disappearance of Kyron, are still ongoing. However, Kyron's whereabouts and the circumstances surrounding his disappearance are still a mystery.

Related: Where Is Casey Anthony Now?

49. The Bizarre Deaths at Dyatlov Pass

On the night of Feb. 1, 1959, nine hikers died mysteriously in the mountains of what is now Russia. On the night of the incident, the group had set up camp on a slope, enjoyed dinner, and got ready for bed but never returned home.

On February 26, a search party found the hikers' abandoned tent, which had been ripped open. Surrounding the area were footprints left by the group, some wearing socks, some wearing a single shoe, some barefoot, all of which followed to the edge of a nearby forest. Two bodies were found there, shoeless and wearing only underwear. Initially, it was believed they died of hypothermia. Still, medical examiners took a look at the body as well as the seven others that were discovered over the months that followed and disproved that theory. One body had evidence of blunt force trauma as the result of a brutal assault, another body had third-degree burns, one had been vomiting blood, and the last one was missing a tongue. Some of their clothing was radioactive.

The morbid theories that floated included KGB interference, drug overdoses, UFOs, gravity anomalies, the Yeti, and a terrifying but real phenomenon called "infrasound," in which the wind interacts with the topography to create a barely audible hum that can induce powerful feelings of nausea, panic, dread, chills, nervousness, raised heart rate and breathing difficulties. The true cause of death for these adventures still remains unsolved.

Craving more true crime? Read up on the mysterious death of Elisa Lam.

9 798889 221000